Cobweb Capers

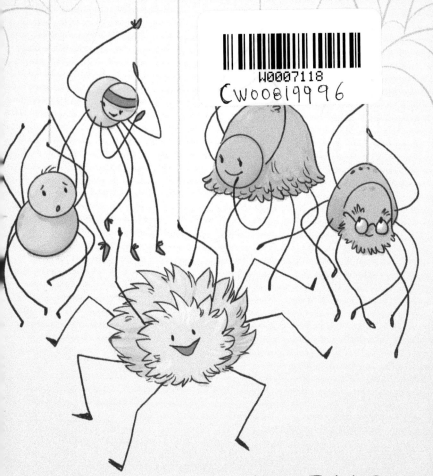

Jane E. McGee

Illustrated by Marisa Lewis

"This book is dedicated to spiders.
Without these fascinating creatures inspiring me
there would be no stories to tell." Jane McGee

Published in the United Kingdom by:

Blue Falcon Publishing
The Mill, Pury Hill Business Park,
Alderton Road, Towcester
Northamptonshire
NN12 7LS
Email: books@bluefalconpublishing.co.uk
Web: www.bluefalconpublishing.co.uk

A CIP record of this book is available from the British Library.

First printed July 2021

ISBN 9781912765362

These children all love spiders!
See what they have to say...

Lauren who is 3 years old has written: "I love spiders because they share my breakfast!" Her spider stickers are on her little table where she eats so she sees them everyday.

Alfie aged 5 who is obsessed with insects has written: "Spiders are special because they are actually really friendly and make really cool webs."

Bonnie aged 8 has written: "I like spiders because they are the only creatures with eight legs."

Luna aged 5 says: "Spiders are special because they make beautiful spiral webs."

George age 4 has written: "I like holding a teeny, tiny, weeny spider. I love spiders."

William age 7 has written: "I like spiders because they eat flies and we take care of spiders and put them somewhere safe."

Samuel aged 8 says: "I love spiders because they are cute and they inspire me to invent things, like things that will help me stick to walls! Whenever I see a spider in my house, I give it a name. Peble, Rocky and Rhodey are my favourite spider pals."

Introducing the Spiders

Mirabelle the
creative spider

Marley the
sensible spider

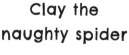

Clay the
naughty spider

AJ the sporty
spider

Orson the
clever spider

Cobweb Capers

Jane E. McGee

Illustrated by Marisa Lewis

The Spider That Came in From the Cold

Five friendly spiders lived in Mr Lee's garden shed. The shed was full of cobwebs because Mr Lee liked spiders. There were cobwebs on the walls, cobwebs on the windows, cobwebs everywhere. It was very messy because Mr Lee was too busy to tidy his shed.

'Brrrr, it's cold outside,' said Marley.

It was getting dark and icicles were starting to form on the windows.

Marley, the sensible spider looked around the shed and could see just two other spiders, Orson and Mirabelle. Orson, the clever spider, who only spoke in rhyme, was reading his favourite book, 'Super Secret Spy-der.'

Mirabelle, the creative spider, was folding a flea and greenfly wrap for her supper. Her webs had the most wonderful patterns, which attracted a large number of insects, which she used for her very tasty insect cakes.

With only three spiders in the shed, this meant that two spiders were still out in the cold. Anjelica, who liked to be called 'AJ', and Clay.

It was getting later and colder. Marley looked out of the window to see if he could see his missing friends.

AJ, the sporty spider, could run faster than most of the male spiders in the area. Clay, the naughty spider, liked to build webs in dangerous places. He also played tricks on the other spiders. A gentle pitter patter of rain sounded on the roof of the shed.

Spiders don't like rain.

Suddenly AJ ran into the shed like an Olympic athlete. 'Maximillian the cat is trying to catch Clay,' she cried, 'we must help Clay at once.' Her voice was trembling and she was shaking.

Maximillian a large, fluffy orange and white cat lived next door with Miss Kelly. He liked to chase and gobble up spiders.

Clay, the naughty spider, had been teasing Maximillian shouting, 'Come and get me!' Maximillian was not a friendly cat. He was getting very angry with Clay.

'Don't worry,' said Marley, 'we need to stay calm and work out a rescue plan.'

'But it's raining,' said Mirabelle, 'we can't go out in the rain, we will be washed away.'

'But we have to do something,' said Marley, 'We can't just leave Clay as Maximillian will catch him!'

'If he catches him he will eat him,' said Mirabelle, 'what are we going to do?'

'I am brave enough to go out in the rain,' said AJ, 'I can spin a long rescue ladder from the shed to the wall and Clay can use it to escape.'

'AJ, it is a great idea, but it will take too long to spin a ladder,' said Marley. 'We must act quickly.'

Suddenly Orson announced a rescue plan:

'I have an idea and that is that
Winifred the hedgehog will save Clay from the cat.
Let's call on Winifred; she will curl into a ball
to distract Maximillian, which will be a relief to us all.
Isn't it a brilliant idea?
I hope I have made myself really clear?'

The spiders were all excited about Orson's rescue plan. The spiders needed to find Winifred and time was running out. It was still raining and Maximillian was still trying to catch Clay.

Orson continued:

'I know it is irritating
that Winifred is hibernating.
We should search high and low
and rescue Clay before the cold wind starts to blow.
If we delay
he will be washed away.'

AJ ran around the shed looking for Winifred.

'Marley you look in the left corner of the shed and I will look to the right,' said AJ.

Orson made a request,

'Mirabelle please make something really yummy,

as Clay will have an empty tummy.'

Mirabelle decided to make Clay's favourite cake, a chocolate bug cake.

Marley ran over to the left corner of the shed. There were a few empty plant pots, a tin of yellow paint with yellow streaks of paints running down the side, a shovel, tin cans, empty jam jars and an old striped deck chair. Marley looked under the deckchair to see if he could find Winifred.

'Winifred, where are you?' shouted AJ, as loud as she could. She wanted to be the first one to find her. AJ always wanted to win.

'I have found Winifred!' announced Marley.

'I knew she would be there under the deckchair,' said Orson.

'Winifred wake up,' shouted Marley.

Winifred did not wake up, she was still sound asleep.

'Let us all shout as loud as we can to wake Winifred,' cried AJ.

The spiders all shouted 'Winifred!' as loud as they could.

Winifred did not wake up, she was still sound asleep.

Orson had another idea:

'The smell of gingerbread
will wake Winifred from her bed,' said Orson.

Mirabelle searched her web for one of her gingerbread moth cakes and waved it under Winifred's nose.

Winifred's nose started to twitch and her eyes began to open.

Winifred rubbed her eyes, 'Hello everyone is it spring yet?'

'No it isn't spring,' said Marley, 'but we need you to spring into action to help Clay.'

'I will help Clay,' said Winifred, 'because he is my friend, you all are!'

'My friend Winifred, there is no time to lose,
so put on your running shoes,' said Orson.

AJ explained the rescue plan to Winifred, who wasted no time. She scurried out of the shed and then she saw Maximillian, his large green eyes were fixed on Clay and his claws were out, ready to pounce.

Maximillian had really sharp claws.

Clay was dangling from his web. Two of his legs hung on to the freezing web for dear life. His six other legs wriggled as he tried to grip the wet wall while the icy wind blew. He looked like a dancing spider.

'Help!' yelled Clay.

Maximillian was glaring at Clay's spider-dance. He was just about to pounce when Winifred rustled past making a snuffling sound.

'What's that going snuffle, snuffle, snuffle?' He wondered. He saw Winifred's prickly shape which moved slowly and surely towards him.

'This should be fun,' said Maximillian, 'this looks like a giant mouse.' Maximillian liked to chase mice.

Maximillian crept over to Winifred who stood very, very still like a statue. Maximillian's paw reached out to touch this strange creature which snuffled. He decided he would like to play, but Winifred was keen to get back to sleep so she slowly curled into a ball.

He decided to take a closer look and put his nose up really close.

'It looks like a mouse with a very thick coat on,' he thought, he went even closer, his whiskers twitched as he sniffed out this creature.

'Ouch!' he cried, 'this ball-shaped-thing is prickly and not very nice at all!' He realised that it was not a large mouse, it was a hedgehog!

While Maximillian was not looking, Clay dropped down from his web and ran as fast as his eight legs would carry him into the safety of the shed. He shouted to Maximillian, 'We fooled you.'

Maximillian did not like being fooled or getting his nose prickled, so his large orange furry shape and sore nose disappeared through the cat flap in Miss Kelly's door. Winifred uncurled herself and shuffled back to the warmth of the shed.

'Phew, that was a close shave, thanks Winfred,' said Clay.

'Clay you must be more careful, we were all really worried about you,' said AJ.

'Can I go back to sleep now?' asked Winifred.

'Thanks Winfred,' shouted the five spiders.

Mirabelle came down from her web and gave Winifred a gingerbread moth and Clay a chocolate bug cake.

'Thanks Mirabelle,' said Clay, 'this looks yummy, my favourite cake, and thanks everyone for helping me.'

Orson had the final word:

'Now Clay my dear friend we know you are bold.

But please remember what you are told and don't stay out so long in the cold. We called on Winifred and she saved the day. Fooled Maximillian and rescued Clay. Three cheers for Winifred, hip hip hurray!'

One Small Step for Spiders

It was a hot and sunny day in June. Mr Lee and his next door neighbour Miss Kelly were talking in the garden.

'Sssshhhh,' said Marley, the sensible spider, he was trying to listen to what they were saying. He had heard the word 'locust.'

Suddenly Mr. Lee came into the shed and placed a poster on the side and then left again.

Marley and the other spiders went to read the poster which said:

MISSING!
FROM DAISY CHAIN SCHOOL

AFRICAN LOCUSTS WITH LARGE APPETITES
RUFUS & TODD
Please help us find them !
REWARD £20

Daisy Chain school were offering a reward of £20.00 for the return of the locusts.

'Locusts are like hungry grasshoppers and Mr Lee will be really worried,' said Marley.

Mr Lee liked to grow all sorts of vegetables and he was very proud of his vegetable plot.

'If the locusts fly into his garden they will eat all of his lettuce and cabbages,' said Marley.

'They will eat his onions,' said Clay.

'They will eat his carrots too,' said AJ.

'It is terrible, two locusts on the loose and hungry ones too,' said Mirabelle.

'Don't worry,' said AJ the sporty spider, 'I am going to catch them in my web.'

'I will catch them first,' said Clay the naughty spider. 'I will trick them into thinking they are flying around happily but they won't see my web and will fly right into it.'

'Oh no they won't,' said AJ.

'Oh yes they will,' said Clay.

'Stop arguing at once,' said Mirabelle, the creative spider, 'we have no time to waste and anyway I have the best and most attractive webs of all. What locust could resist my web?'

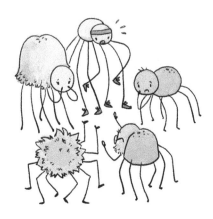

Orson, who only spoke in rhyme said,

'We have no time to rest

we must all do our best

to put these two locusts under arrest

Because they are such a pest

We must stay focussed

if we want to catch the locusts.'

'If we catch the locusts then kind old Mr Lee will get his reward of £20.00 from Daisy Chain school,' said Mirabelle.

'We must make sure the locusts survive because they will be worth far more money alive

Build your webs with care

and give the locusts a nasty scare,' said Orson.

'We must try and build our webs where the locusts may fly, by the lettuce and cabbage,' said Marley.

The spiders got to work right away building their webs in places where the locusts may land, but Mirabelle who didn't like going outside decided to build her web in the shed.

Todd and Rufus had escaped from Daisy Chain school. They planned to eat as much as they could in order to fly back to Africa to join the other locusts who lived there. Africa was a long way. They would stop on the way to feed.

Their flight path was taking them over Miss Kelly's garden when they saw some ripe red strawberries on the kitchen window.

'Hey, Rufus look at those strawberries!' said Todd.

'They look yummy,' said Rufus.

The window was open and the locusts flew straight onto the ripe strawberries.

Miss Kelly's cat, Maximillian, was in the kitchen and heard a buzzing sound made by Todd and Rufus and decided to get a better look. Maximillian jumped onto the kitchen sink and knocked over a small plate which smashed onto the floor.

'Max, is that you making that noise?' asked Miss Kelly.

She went into the kitchen to see what had smashed onto the kitchen floor and saw the locusts on her strawberries.

She screamed. Maximillian tried to catch the locusts with his paw, but they were too quick. They flew away.

'Look there's a shed over there, let's hide in there,' said Rufus.

Rufus and Todd flew into Mr Lee's shed and straight into Mirabelle's invisible web. She was famous in the area for her invisible webs.

'I've caught them,' said Mirabelle! She was very, very excited.

The other spiders ran into the shed to see the locusts. Todd and Rufus, were struggling to get out of Mirabelle's web.

'I have made it with special thread,' said Mirabelle, 'you won't be able to escape.'

'But you will survive
and be captured alive,' said Orson.

'Let us go,' said Rufus, 'we are hungry and we are going back to Africa.'

'I feel sorry for them,' said Clay 'shall we let them go?'

'No,' said Marley, 'they will eat all of these vegetables if you let them go. They belong to the school.

The children from the school are missing them and

want them back.'

Mr Lee ran into the shed, Miss Kelly had told him she had seen the locusts flying in there. He saw them in Mirabelle's web, took them out carefully and placed them in an empty jam jar ready to take back to the school.

The spiders were thrilled that Mr Lee would now get his reward of £20.00 from the school.

'We have caught them thanks to the spider's webs,' said Mr Lee.

'I bet he will use his reward to buy some new vegetables and some strawberries for Miss Kelly,' said Marley.

Orson had the final word:

'Mirabelle's web has saved the day

Three cheers for Mirabelle hip hip hurray.'

The Spiders Who Loved Me

Mirabelle the creative spider was giving her web a spring clean when she saw her calendar. She gasped, 'Oh No!'

It was Winifred the Hedgehog's birthday in 2 days' time.

Winifred was a very good friend to all of the spiders and they always gave her a present for her birthday.

Mirabelle looked around the shed for the four other spiders.

Orson was writing his latest poem.

The other spiders Marley, AJ and Clay were building their webs outside. It was a warm spring day and lots of insects were flying around. Mirabelle called to the other spiders to come into the shed at once.

'It is Winifred's birthday in two days' time,' said Mirabelle, 'we must make her something special as she is always helping us.'

Orson who only spoke in rhyme said:

'We must make haste
There is no time to waste
I have a good plan
We should catch as many insects as we can
Then you can make
The most splendid cake.'

'That's a wonderful idea,' said Marley.

Clay the naughty spider said, 'Winifred's favourite food is moths and I know just where to build my web to catch the most moths. I will build my web at the top of the lamp post, moths like the light and I can catch lots of moths up there.'

AJ the sporty spider wanted to be the one who caught the most insects and decided that the best place was in next door neighbour Miss Kelly's summer house.

Marley decided to build his web near the wasp nest. Wyman, a very fierce wasp was in charge of a colony of wasps who had made a nest under Mr Lee's roof and with the warm spring sunshine they had started to get more lively.

Orson decided that he would write a poem for Winifred's birthday but before he did he gave the spiders strict instructions.

'Be kind to the butterflies and the bees,
They are good for the plants and trees,
But wasps are so fierce
Their stings they do pierce.
Wyman's wasps are really vicious,
But don't forget they taste really delicious.
Insects will fly into your webs and get stuck,
So my friends go to work and I wish you good luck.'

Clay then saw a wooden telephone pole where he could get a better grip. This would have to do.

Clay climbed higher and higher, but froze when he

saw Claude, the fierce large black crow, at the top of the pole.

Crows like to eat spiders.

Clay kept very still until Claude the crow flew away.

Clay would catch more moths at night but this meant that AJ and Marley had a head start.

Marley had already caught two wasps in his web and AJ had caught three flies.

Clay decided to climb down and build his web near the compost heap where there were lots of flying insects to catch.

Suddenly Fuzzy-Buzzy the bumblebee flew past.

'Hello, Marley,' she said, 'What are you up to?'

'I am catching flies for Winfred's birthday,' said Marley 'Mirabelle is making a pie with all of the insects.'

'That's a nice idea,' said Fuzzy-Buzzy, 'I could get you some honey if you wish.'

'That would be great,' said Marley.

The spiders were busy all day and all night catching the different insects for Winifred's birthday cake.

Mirabelle worked her magic and made the most wonderful layer cake with flies moths and wasps. She called the cake the 'Beautiful bug pie.'

As promised, Fuzzy-Buzzy brought some honey which she had made.

'I will go and find Winfred,' said AJ.

The spiders wished Winfred Happy Birthday and when she saw the cake she was really pleased.

'I will invite all my hedgehog friends to help me eat this cake, it looks like the best cake ever, it looks really yummy.'

Orson had the final word —
'We wish you the happiest birthday
And hope you have a wonderful day.
Three cheers for Winifred hip hip hurray!'

Two Flew Over
The Dragonfly's Nest

Clay the naughty spider decided that he wanted to fly.

He had seen Wyman and his colony of wasps fly and it looked so much fun.

Wyman's wasps could buzz around Max the cat's head and he couldn't catch them. Buddy the dragonfly had beautiful peacock blue wings and flew all over the ponds and fields catching insects all day.

Chloe the beautiful white butterfly flapped her white wings and flew so gracefully.

Clay decided that he wanted to fly and he would ask Buddy and Chloe to give him flying lessons.

Clay told the other spiders that he was going to learn how to fly.

'If I could fly I could travel far and wide catching insects and I could see the world from the air.'

'But we are spiders,' said Marley, 'spiders can't fly, we can only dangle from our webs.'

'Marley is right,' said Mirabelle, 'we can't fly because we don't have any wings.'

AJ the sporty spider always wanted to win and she decided that she would also learn to fly but she would be quicker and better at flying than Clay.

'I am going to make some wings,' said Clay, 'Buddy the Dragonfly and Chloe the butterfly are going to give me flying lessons.'

'If I have wings I will be able to fly and Maximillian the cat will not be able to catch me.'

AJ said, 'I will also learn to fly but I will be able to fly much better than Clay.'

'Oh no you won't,' said Clay.

'Oh yes I will,' said AJ.

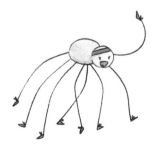

Orson the clever spider said,
'You can both give it a try,
To see if you are able to fly.
Your wings will need to be large and light
And this will help you to take flight.'
Marley helped AJ collect some large white daisy petals which she would use for her wings.
Mirabelle would weave the petals onto AJ and Clay. The petals would look like wings.

Marley then helped Clay to collect some wings that looked like Buddy the Dragonfly. They found some blue bells but they were a bit heavy, but they were blue so they would have to do.

When the spiders had their flower petals attached they were ready.

Buddy the Dragonfly showed Clay how to take off.

'It is easy,' said Buddy, 'you just flap your wings and you will fly into the air.'

Buddy flapped his peacock blue wings really fast and he was off.

Now it was Clay's turn.

'Go on, Clay you can do it,' said Marley.

'Three cheers for Clay,' said Mirabelle.

Clay ran along the shelf as fast has he could and when he got to the end he flapped his blue bell wings as fast as he could but instead of flying he started to fall and fall quickly. To stop himself he started to spin a thread as quickly as he could to avoid hitting the floor.

Orson said,

'That was a good first try,

Even though you did not fly.

You did not even hit the ground,

So you are back safe and sound.'

Clay was very disappointed but he wanted to try again.

Buddy the Dragonfly said, 'Clay all you need is practise, don't give up.'

Now it was AJ's turn.

'Go on, AJ you can do it,' said Marley.

'Three cheers for AJ,' said Mirabelle.

AJ's white flower petal wings were lighter than Clay's bluebell wings and she was confident that she would be able to float and fly like Chloe the white butterfly.

'AJ just flap your wings like me and you will be able

to float into the air,' said Chloe.

AJ ran along the top shelf in the shed and when she got to the end she flapped her flower petal wings like Chloe the beautiful white butterfly.

But just like Clay instead of flying she fell like a stone and stopped herself by spinning some web thread.

Orson made a suggestion.
'That was a good first try, AJ and Clay,
But in order for you to fly away,
You need some wind, a little breeze,
So have another try if you please.'

Clay decided to run along the shelf and out of the window where it was breezy and flap his wings and that may help him to fly.

He watched Buddy fly out of the shed window with his beautiful peacock blue wings.

'Better luck this time,' said Marley.

'Good luck Clay,' said Mirabelle.

But Clay couldn't fly. His bluebell wings did not hover like Buddy's wings.

AJ tried again she sailed out of the window, floated a little like Chloe the butterfly, but then she fell like a stone.

Clay and AJ tried and tried again but they still could not fly.

'Never mind,' said Marley. 'Not everyone is able to fly, humans have been trying for years to fly like birds and even humans can't fly!'

'Yes, you can fly,' said Buddy. 'Come on Clay, hop on I will take you over the pond.'

'Come on, AJ,' said Chloe hold tight and we can fly over the fields.

So Clay and AJ had a really fun afternoon flying with Buddy and Chloe.

Afterwards Clay said, 'That was great fun I still wish I could fly but I will have to be happy being a spider.'

Chloe said, 'I may be able to fly but I can't weave webs like you. I really wish I could have a nice web to live in because I don't have a proper home. At night I hang from the undersides of leaves, or crawl into crevices in the bark of trees.'

'I don't have a web to live in either,' said Buddy.

Clay and AJ decided that it wasn't that bad being a spider and decided not to get in a spin about flying again.

Orson had the final word.

'Although it would be nice to fly,

I have learned as time has gone by

Butterflies may be beautiful but spiders are gallant.

We can weave our webs and that is our own special talent.'

Spoil Sport Spiders

It was a week before the Spider Olympics when all of the spiders in town went to the summer house in Miss Kelly's garden to compete.

The winning spider in each event would win a supply of insects to keep a spider fed for 7 days.

The events this year were:

Web weaving.

Insect catching.

Painting.

Running and jumping.

Orson and his friend Blake were judging the events.

AJ was competing in the running event and had been practising for a week now and she was ready for the three metre race.

'I can run faster than most spiders,' said AJ, 'I always come first.'

Even Clay the naughty spider decided not to try to beat AJ because he knew that she could run faster than him.

Mirabelle always came first in the web weaving competition, because her webs had the most wonderful designs and many spiders wished that they could weave a web as fine as Mirabelle.

Marley decided to enter the insect catching competition as he was sensible and knew just were to build his web to catch the most insects.

Clay was still deciding which event he would compete in.

'Which competition are you going to enter this year, Clay?' asked Marley.

'I think I am going to have a go at painting, I have 8 legs and I should be good at painting a picture.

I think I am going to paint a picture of sunflowers. I can hold a brush in each leg and it won't take long to paint the petals.'

Clay looked around Mr Lee's shed to see if he could see some paint he wanted to practise before the big day.

Mirabelle was also practising for the big day by weaving many cobwebs to get the design just right.

A group of rival spiders also wanted to win the insect prize and were plotting to cheat in order to win first prize in the painting and running events. This group of 4 spiders were called 'The Zappers' and they were very naughty. Their leader was called Zorko who was the biggest cheat of all.

The next day all of the spiders were ready for the events and started to head towards Miss Kelly's summer house.

Orson was at the door to meet all of the spiders who were taking part in the activities.

When all the spiders were in the summer house Orson said:

'Hello, everyone

We are gathered here today for this really big event

So I hope that it will be time well spent.

I hope you don't come unstuck

so I wish you all good luck,' he said.

There were 40 spiders altogether and it was really big event.

'Oh no,' said AJ, 'Zorko and his team The Zappers are here and they don't like us.'

'Orson and Blake please can you send the The Zappers and Zorko away? They always try to cheat, we don't like them and they don't like us,' said Mirabelle.

Orson said
'We have to include them just to be fair
Try to ignore them
Pretend that you don't care.
AJ always wins her race
so just try and focus and put on a brave face.'
'I agree,' said Marley, 'let's be positive, we are spiders and we are united.'
'Here here,' said Clay, 'we will show The Zappers who are the best at all of the events.'

AJ got ready for the race and she was racing against 4 other spiders and she was really excited about the chance of winning.

AJ had to run for 3 meters until the winning post.

But Zorko had put a small obstacle in her way towards the winning post to trip AJ, so she would loose and one of The Zappers would win.

'The whistle I will blow.
'Now ready steady go,' shouted Orson.
'Hurray for AJ,' shouted Mirabelle.

The spiders were off and AJ got off to a flying start she saw Marley at the end of the race cheering her.

Marley looked on the track and saw a small obstacle and AJ was running right towards it. Marley quickly moved it out of the way just in the nick of time and AJ was able to win her race and was first past the post.

'Hurray for AJ,' shouted Orson.

Sensible Marley had moved the obstacle and he had an idea that it was one of The Zappers who had placed it there to stop AJ from winning. But it wasn't over yet.

Clay was missing.

Mirabelle had started her web spinning competition so AJ and Marley decided to look for Clay. They went towards the paint tins at the back of the summer house, and they could hear a muffled cry for help.

'That's Clay,' said Marley.

'Clay where are you?' shouted AJ.

'Over here,' came the cry.

'It's coming from over there,' said Marley, pointing to a tin.' Look there's a tin of yellow paint,' said AJ.

Marley and AJ were shocked to find Clay swimming in the yellow paint and he couldn't get out.

'Help get me out,' cried Clay.

'Marley and AJ started spinning some web thread to help Clay get out of the paint. They managed to rescue him just in time before he sank in the yellow paint.

'You look funny,' said AJ laughing, 'you have turned yellow.'

'Stop laughing,' said Clay, 'it isn't funny, one of The Zappers pushed me in the tin so they could win the painting competition.'

Orson was just about to award the first prize in the painting competition to Zorko.

'He can't win!' said Marley. 'He cheated, we must do something at once.'

Just before Orson handed the first prize to Zorko Clay shouted 'Stop!'

The audience looked at this strange yellow spider and all stated to laugh very loudly.

Orson turned to Clay and asked.

'Hello, Clay my dear fellow
Why are you yellow?'

'It is from the tin of yellow paint,' said Clay.

'How did you get in the paint tin, did you fall in?' asked Orson.

'No I was pushed in to the tin of paint by Zorko from The Zappers so he could win first prize,' said Clay. 'If Marley and AJ hadn't rescued me I would have drowned!'

All of the audience gasped in horror.

'It wasn't me,' said Zorko. 'He's lying.'

Marley said, 'Zorko and his team also tried to trip AJ by putting an obstacle in her way to trip her over, but luckily I saw it first.'

Blake shook his head in horror and so did Orson. 'This is very serious,' said Blake.

'Because you have lied
you are all disqualified!' said Orson.

The audience cheered Orson, and then booed Zorko and his team, The Zappers,

who ran out of the summer house in disgrace.

The audience shouted, 'Give the first prize to the yellow spider!'

So the spider Olympics was over for another year, AJ came first in the race and Mirabelle in her web weaving competition. Not forgetting Marley who caught the most insects in his web.

'I knew we were the best,' said Marley, 'we won our prizes without cheating.' Orson had the final word.

'I am sorry to report
that Zorko and his team spoiled the sport,
but fair play won the day,
three cheers for the winners.
Hip Hip Hurray.'

Wishing on a Starfish

The five spiders were spending a lazy Sunday afternoon in Mr Lee's shed.

It was early autumn and despite the pale sunbeam shining in through the window of the shed, there was a chill in the autumn air. Orson, Marley, AJ and Clay were feeling very content.

Mirabelle, on the other hand, wasn't pleased.

She wanted to be somewhere warm and sunny.

Mirabelle looked over the shed to a small bench by the window and saw the pale afternoon sun shining on a mysterious glitter globe.

Mirabelle was curious to find out more and so she scuttled off to take a closer look. Mirabelle looked inside the glitter globe and saw a soft sandy beach, a large green palm trees a Mermaid, a star fish, deck chairs and beach huts merging into a sparkling turquoise blue sea.

Under the glitter globe, in pretty, purple, sparkly letters, was written:

'Count to ten and make a wish!'

'One, two, three, four, five, six, seven, eight, nine, ten!' Mirabelle counted excitedly. Mirabelle closed her eyes and wished that she was somewhere as sunny as the glorious glitter globe. She opened one of her eyes: nothing seemed to have happened.

Convinced it was all a trick, she fell soundly asleep next to the glitter globe, her dreams filled with visions of exotic islands — sand, sun and sea — just like she had wished for.

Mirabelle woke from her sleep to the sound of gentle waves and birds singing. She couldn't believe it. She was on a beautiful, sandy beach. In the distance, there was a large boat on top of the sea, some small beach huts, and a large palm tree on the horizon.

Mirabelle continued to scan her surroundings, and began to walk through the sand, leaving eight little footprints behind her with each step.

Mirabelle decided to take a look around to see if she could see any people or any other spiders. Maybe they are having a little nap in the afternoon because it is so warm here she thought.

Mirabelle looked around, she peered in the beech huts and looked under the deck chairs but couldn't see any people.

Mirabelle went from beach hut to beach hut looking for spiders but still couldn't find anyone.

She started to get very warm. The weather was scorching, just as she had wished for but she was starting to wonder whether what she had wished for was actually a huge mistake. She had to use one of her eight legs to wipe a bead of sweat from her brow.

'It's too hot in here!' Mirabelle cried.

I want to go home, back to Mr Lee's shed to see the other spiders, AJ, Clay, Marley and Orson. She started to walk but hit a glass wall. 'Oh no,' gasped Mirabelle, 'I am trapped in the glitter globe.'

She peered out of the globe and saw Mr Lee's shed and plant pots and the other spiders hanging in their webs.

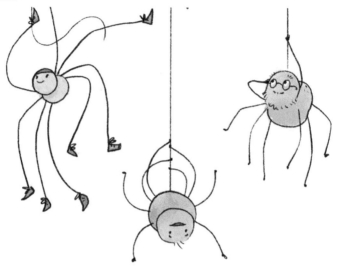

She shouted 'Help!' hoping the other spiders could see and hear her but it was no use. They could not hear her cries for help.

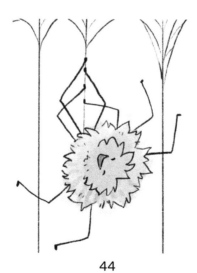

Mirabelle walked slowly across the beach and drank desperately from the salty sea water, trying to find any way she could cool herself down.

Terrified that she would be stuck in the glitter globe forever, Mirabelle lay quietly in the sand, unsure of what to do next.

All of a sudden, there was a loud swish and a splash. Out of the sea rose a magnificent mermaid, covered in shiny scales, which shone brightly in the golden sunlight rays.

Mirabelle was startled by the Mermaid and approached the beautiful creature in the water. 'Hello Miss Mermaid, please help me! I am very lost and I just want to go home.' Mirabelle cried out. The magnificent Mermaid looked concerned. The Mermaid shook both her head and her tail at Mirabelle.

'I'm so sorry, I wish I could help you, but I don't know how.' She paused for a moment, thinking.

'I do know that the starfish knows the way. If you ask the starfish, I'm sure she will gladly tell you how to get back home.' A gentle voice replied.

The mermaid smiled warmly and nodded her head towards a smiling starfish on the golden sand just behind Mirabelle.

'Thank you so much Miss Mermaid!' she gratefully replied.

Mirabelle raced up to the happy starfish and said, 'Please help me I am lost and I want to go home.'

'How did you get in here?' asked the starfish.

'I counted to ten and I made a wish,' said Mirabelle.

'Well then it is easy,' said the starfish, 'close your eyes and count back from 10 to 1 and make a wish. You see counting backwards will get you back to where you want to be.'

Mirabelle, closed her eyes and counted, 'ten, nine, eight, seven, six, five, four, three, two, one ... I wish I were back in Mr Lee's old garden shed with the other spiders.'

Mirabelle opened her eyes and she was back in the shed and was immediately pleased to see no tropical island, no scorching sun, no enormous palm trees but her favourite old garden shed, where she knew she was destined to be all along.

'Where have you been?' asked AJ.

'We have been looking for you,' said Clay.

'I knew that you would come back,' said Marley.

Mirabelle went to see the glitter globe just to take another look. AJ, Clay, Marley and Orson followed her.

When she looked everything looked the same. The magnificent mermaid, the smiley starfish and the shimmering turquoise sea, just as she remembered.

Then she looked more closely and she could see eight fresh footprints in the sand which she was sure weren't there before.

AJ and Clay also looked into the glitter globe.

'Isn't it pretty?' said Marley, 'I wish I could walk along that sparkling sandy beach.'

'I would like to build my web up that palm tree,' said Clay.

'I would love to dip one of my eight legs in that sparkling sea,' said AJ.

'I prefer to be here with my friends,' said Mirabelle. 'There aren't any spiders in the glitter globe and you would be very lonely.'

'A pale blue sky, a turquoise sea

A pretty mermaid, a green palm tree

A sandy beach upon which to roam

It may look like paradise but it doesn't look like home!'

Said Orson.

Mirabelle smiled, she was pleased she was back on the other side of the glitter globe with her friends even if it wasn't warm and sunny.

'There really is no place like home,' chuckled Mirabelle. 'Even if it is a cold shed!'

About the Author

Dr Jane McGee works as a teacher of Psychology. The idea for her spider stories developed after she took a group of her students to a spider phobia workshop. The students, were initially afraid of spiders all volunteered up to handle the Chilean Rose Tarantula at the end of the session. This demonstrates that familiarity can reduce fears and even increase a liking of spiders. Jane decided to write this series of spider stories for children in the hope it would encourage them to see these fascinating creatures in a more favourable light. Spiders are a vital part of the ecosystem but unfortunately they often killed for no reason except irrational fear. The 'Cobweb Capers' stories show these little guys are full of personality, much like the cats and dogs we share our homes with! Find out more about Jane at www.cobwebcapers.com.

About the Illustrator

Marisa Lewis has a Master's degree in Creative Digital Media, and a passion for books and art. By day, she works as an editor at 3dtotal Publishing, creating books and resources for students and professional artists in the entertainment industry.

About Buglife

Buglife is the only organisation in Europe devoted to the conservation of all invertebrates. They are actively working to save Britain's rarest little animals, everything from bees to beetles, worms to woodlice, and jumping spiders to jellyfish. There are more than 40,000 invertebrate species in the UK, and many of these are under threat as never before. As Sir David Attenborough says: "If we and the rest of the back-boned animals were to disappear over night, the rest of the world would get on pretty well. But if invertebrates were to disappear, the worlds eco-systems would collapse."
30% of net sales will go to Buglife.

Unscramble

Help AJ unscramble her friend's names!

_____

L   Y   C   A

_____

S   N   O   R   O

_____

Y   R   A   E   L   M

_____

R   L   M   A   E   B   L   I   E

_____

Quick Quiz

From the story, how many insect cakes does
Mirabelle need to make for the other spider?
From the story, how many winter socks does
Orson need to keep his feet warm, answer?

A: How many insect cakes does Mirabelle need to make for the other spider - 4
A: How many winter socks does Orson need to keep his feet warm, answer - 8

Spot the Difference

There are five (5) differences to find

Help the Spiders get Back to their Webs!

Lightning Source UK Ltd.
Milton Keynes UK
UKHW020751140721
387139UK00007B/99